This edition published by Parragon Books Ltd in 2015
and distributed by

Parragon Inc.
440 Park Avenue South, 13th Floor
New York, NY 10016
www.parragon.com

Copyright © Parragon Books Ltd 2014–2015
Text © Hollins University

Written by Margaret Wise Brown
Illustrated by Alessandra Psacharopulo

ISBN 978-1-4748-1347-1

Printed in China

Jingle Paws

PaRragon

Bath · New York · Cologne · Melbourne · Delhi
Hong Kong · Shenzhen · Singapore · Amsterdam

It was quiet in the house.

Quiet as a tangerine.

Quiet as a nut.

Quiet as cranberry sauce.

When all of a sudden,
At the sound of a mouse—

Squeak!

Cat leapt from the bed

And ran through the house.

Where could the mouse be?

Cat wanted a chase—

Down the stairs,

under chairs,

And in every fun place.

Cat crept in the closet

And took a close look.

He searched every corner—
Each cranny and nook.

At a noise from the chimney
Cat hid by the tree.

It seemed loud for a mouse,
So what could it be?

Cat peeked out for a look,
But this was no mouse—
A dog with his helpers

whooshed

into the house.

Cat's eyes opened wide—
It was **Jingle Paws!**

With a sack full of presents—
Like a pets' Santa Claus!

There were gifts for the pets:
For the mouse, a ripe cheese,
And cat's favorite—catnip!
(Though the toy made him sneeze!)

Jingle Paws found some treats
Left for him by the grate,

And he ate them right up,
Licking crumbs from the plate!

Then he wagged his short tail—
It was time to move on.

With a **whoosh** up the chimney
And a **woof**, he was gone!

Cat was ready to play,   When who should he see?

But a mouse eating cheese,
Right there in the tree!

And for the rest of the night
There was peace in the house,

As, under the tree,
Cat played with a mouse.